Beast Quest®

LycaxA
HUNTER OF THE PEAKS

BY ADAM BLADE

With special thanks to Tabitha Jones

www.beastquest.co.uk

ORCHARD BOOKS

First published in Great Britain in 2020 by The Watts Publishing Group

1 3 5 7 9 10 8 6 4 2

A CIP catalogue record for this book is available from the British Library.

ISBN 978 1 40836 186 3

Printed in Great Britain

The paper and board used in this book are made from wood from responsible sources

Orchard Books
An imprint of Hachette Children's Group
Part of The Watts Publishing Group Limited
Carmelite House, 50 Victoria Embankment, London EC4Y 0DZ

An Hachette UK Company
www.hachette.co.uk
www.hachettechildrens.co.uk

Welcome to the world of Beast Quest!

Tom was once an ordinary village boy, until he travelled to the City, met King Hugo and discovered his destiny. Now he is the Master of the Beasts, sworn to defend Avantia and its people against Evil. Tom draws on the might of the magical Golden Armour, and is protected by powerful tokens granted to him by the Good Beasts of Avantia. Together with his loyal companion Elenna, Tom is always ready to visit new lands and tackle the enemies of the realm.

While there's blood in his veins, Tom will never give up the Quest...

THE LABYRINTH JUNGLE
THE PEAKS OF DESPAIR

DANGER
DEATH
ZARGON'S
PRISON
HE MOAT OF
VAKUNDA

There are special gold coins to collect in this book. You will earn one coin for every chapter you read.

Find out what to do with your coins at the end of the book.

CONTENTS

When my aunt Aroha left Tangala to marry King Hugo of Avantia, I thought I could rule this kingdom. I wanted to make her proud, to protect the country's borders and keep my people safe.

I have failed. The sorcerer who took me claims to be hundreds of years old. He says he will not kill me, if my aunt does the right thing. It's the Jewels of Tangala that he wants. A simple swap – me for the magical stones. But if Aroha delivers them, the results will be far worse than one death. All Tangala will be in peril. My only hope is that my aunt has some other plan, some way to rescue me, but save the kingdom too.

She will need brave heroes at her side if she is to succeed.

Rotu

Regent of Tangala, and nephew to the queen.

ZARGON RETURNS

Tom gazed about in wonder at the lush undergrowth as he and Elenna trudged through the Labyrinth Jungle. Queen Aroha walked ahead of them with Yara, one of her most trusted warriors. Morning sunlight cast golden shafts through mist rising from the earth all around them. Its warmth eased Tom's muscles, stiff from a night spent sleeping on the ground. Colourful butterflies and tiny birds, no bigger than bees, flitted between flowers, and silver-blue fish splashed in the babbling stream at their side. Tom plucked a peach from a low-hanging branch and sank his teeth into its sweet golden flesh.

"This is good!" he said, wiping juice from his chin.

Elenna popped the last grape from the bunch she'd been eating into her mouth. "When it's not trying to kill us, Vakunda's a paradise!" she said once she'd finished. "Maybe the whole of the kingdom will be as beautiful as this after we've defeated the other three Beasts that guard it."

"We can only hope so," Queen Aroha said, hurrying onwards without looking back. "But remember, we're here to find Rotu, and bring him home alive."

Tom, Elenna and the queen had already battled Akorta, a giant ape-Beast, on the first stage of their Quest to rescue Aroha's nephew from the Evil Wizard, Zargon. Upon the Beast's demise, the overgrown jungle of Zargon's cursed kingdom had begun to transform. Trees, which only yesterday had been tangled with snaking vines, were now bowed beneath the weight of ripe fruit.

Their once silent branches rustled with life.

"Personally, I can't wait to get out of here," Yara muttered, swatting at

a mosquito. The Tangalan warrior had been Prince Rotu's bodyguard at the time of his capture and had volunteered to help with his rescue. "If it isn't an outsized monkey trying to eat us alive, it's the insects!"

Tom finished his peach and stooped to rinse his sticky hands in the cool water of the stream. He rose to join the others as they walked through a leafy curtain of vegetation and stopped in the bright sunshine of a grassy plain.

Once Tom's eyes had adjusted, his spirits plummeted. An immense mountain range spanned the horizon, climbing in a series of jagged peaks to blade-like summits that jutted

into the clear blue sky.

"The Peaks of Despair," Queen Aroha said. "They used to be known as the Hills of Plenty, but they changed when the Jewels of Tangala were taken back from Zargon. No one has set foot on these mountains

for five hundred years."

"I'm not sure we should chance our luck either," Elenna said, frowning up at the snow-capped peaks. "We've only got one rope. Is there any way around the mountains?"

"Perhaps you should return to

Avantia…" Yara said, scowling, "…if you're *afraid.*"

Elenna rounded on the woman, her cheeks flushing as if she'd been slapped.

"There's no point risking our necks if we don't have to," she said. "After all, if we fall to our deaths, there won't be anyone left to save Prince Rotu."

Her eyes cold and hard, Yara opened her mouth to speak, but Aroha cut her off.

"Peace!" the queen said, sharply. "Crossing the mountains will be dangerous. But look…" She opened her map and gestured to a ring of mountains surrounded by a jungle.

"Just like the Labyrinth Jungle, they form a ring. The only way to get to Zargon's island at the centre is to climb. And we will have to work together if we mean to reach the other side alive."

Yara quickly bowed her head. "Of course, my queen," she said.

"I'm sorry, Your Majesty," Elenna muttered, her cheeks glowing even redder.

Queen Aroha turned on her heel and struck off towards the mountains. Tom started after her, but a sudden flash of white light made him reel back, blinded. He blinked hard to find the shimmering image of a tall, muscular man clad

in black wizard's robes standing before them, his tanned arms folded across his chest. A clipped beard and moustache surrounded his thin lips, which were drawn back in a sneer of distaste. His curled hair showed no hint of white and his skin was smooth, but somehow his hooded grey eyes looked as old and as uncaring as mountains themselves. As Tom met the wizard's pitiless gaze, he suppressed a shudder. It felt like staring into the eyes of a venomous snake.

"Zargon!" Aroha gasped, flinching back from the vision, but then she drew herself tall. "Where is Rotu?" she demanded.

A smile played at the corners of the wizard's lips. "He is safe. For now..." he said, then lifted a black-gloved hand, turning it towards the sun so that a gold ring worn over the leather caught the light.

"That's Rotu's!" Aroha cried.

Yara stepped towards Zargon's smirking image, her fists balled. "If any harm has come to him, I'll—"

"I assure you," Zargon cut in, "it is in Rotu's best interests – in fact, it's in the best interests of all the known kingdoms – that you leave the four Jewels of Tangala where you stand and depart at once. I have had centuries to consider my revenge – enough time to discover many new ways of inflicting pain on my enemies."

Zargon's image flared bright, then vanished.

Aroha turned to the others, her face pale. "Seeing Zargon is like a nightmare brought to life," she said. "His name alone used to be enough to keep even the most unruly children in bed. And now my nephew is in his clutches...at his mercy!"

The sight of Aroha's anguished expression filled Tom with new resolve. "While there's blood in my veins, I will fight Zargon and his Beasts," he told her. "I won't rest until Rotu has been freed!"

"I don't think fighting will help the

prince," Yara said. "You heard what Zargon said. The only way to save him now is to surrender the jewels. And what do we care about Vakunda, anyway? It's a desolate land that means nothing to us. I say, we should leave Zargon to his precious kingdom if it means bringing Rotu home alive."

"Now who's afraid?" Elenna cried. "We can't just give up!"

"I'm not giving up!" Yara snapped. Then she turned to Queen Aroha. "I'll take the jewels to Zargon myself, and escort Rotu back to you. I feel it is only right that I shoulder this responsibility, since I was the one tasked with keeping Rotu safe in the first place. Your Majesty, I must put right my mistake."

Queen Aroha shook her head. "I appreciate your dedication to my nephew," she said, "but we cannot let Evil prevail. And I am no fool. Zargon has every reason to hate Tangala. If he gets his hands on the jewels, he will be too powerful for us to fight. He will set his evil loose in Tangala, and Avantia after that. Vakunda does indeed mean something to us now. Zargon must be stopped, once and for all. We have to defeat him."

Tom nodded, swallowing hard. "Aroha's right," he told Yara. "If you give Zargon what he wants, he will most likely still kill you and Rotu anyway. We must find a way to rescue the prince without parting with the jewels..." He glanced up at the colossal peaks ranged ahead, feeling a chill run through his heart. "Even if it means risking our lives on the Peaks of Despair."

1

THE TUNNEL

Tom shaded his eyes against the glare of the sun and gazed up at the rugged slopes before them, trying to pick out a route over the mountains. Up close, the Peaks of Despair looked more formidable than ever. Loose scree covered the steep foothills, while sharp ridges and deep crevasses scored the higher slopes. Near the top, peak after jagged peak rose one after another into the distance, some almost vertical and many tipped with snow and ice. Tom couldn't see any sign of birds or animals living amongst the barren rocks. Not even a stunted bush. *Just like the Labyrinth Jungle before the defeat of Akorta*, he thought, as a prickle of dread ran over his skin. The air was utterly still, and the silence so complete it seemed to press on his eardrums.

"I'll lead the way," Queen Aroha said, striking off over the uneven ground, the clatter of her footsteps echoing.

"Yara, you and Elenna go before

me," Tom told the others. "That way, if anyone falls, I may be able to use Arcta's eagle feather to save them."

Yara nodded and started after the queen. Casting one last look up at the perilous climb ahead, Elenna squared her shoulders, then set off after the warrior woman.

Loose chunks of stone shifted beneath Tom's feet as he climbed, so that for every two steps forwards, he seemed to slide one step back. Even sound-looking rocks twisted treacherously beneath his feet, pitching him on to his hands and knees. As the sun climbed higher and the morning grew steadily hotter, his leg muscles ached with the effort of keeping his footing. Sweat stung his eyes, making his vision blur, and his breath came fast and ragged in the thin air.

At the sound of a gasp from above, Tom blinked the burning sweat from his eyes to see Yara and Aroha at a ledge, frowning down at something near their feet. Through his blurred vision, he could just make out what looked like yellowed bone…teeth… the hollow eye-sockets of a skull. Elenna looked down at him, worry in her eyes, before she turned and climbed faster, joining Yara and the queen.

As he joined them on the ledge, Tom recognised the bones as the

remains of a horned animal – possibly a goat. The creature's skull lay smashed in brittle fragments, but Tom couldn't see a rock large enough to have caused such damage nearby.

"What Beast lives in these

mountains?" he asked Aroha.

The queen glanced about, wary. "The legends tell of Lycaxa: a wild, rabid dog, with teeth like shards of sharpened rock, and paws large enough to crush his prey. He is said to move as quietly as the mist..."

"Then let's hope we don't meet him on the mountain," Tom said, his eyes on the shattered skull.

Elenna nodded. "This climb will be hard enough without a crazed predator to worry about."

The sun beat down on Tom's back with the dry, relentless heat of a forge as they climbed higher, the way growing steeper with each step. Scrambling up a sharp incline covered in scree, he heard a clatter from above, just before Yara cried, "Look out!"

Tom glanced up to see a huge chunk of dislodged rock coming straight for his head. He managed to duck aside just in time. The queen's warrior gave him a sheepish wave.

As they left the stony foothills behind them, their route only became more treacherous, with almost vertical walls of rock blocking their path. Tom climbed hand over hand, wedging his fingers and toes into any tiny cracks that he could find. Sweat made Tom's grip slippery, and no matter how much water he drank, his throat felt parched.

Stopping on a narrow shelf for yet another swig, Tom noticed his canteen was now more than half empty. He glanced up at the knife-like summits, still far above them, and his shoulders slumped. They barely seemed any closer.

Tom turned to Elenna. "I don't think our water's going to last."

Elenna tipped a trickle of water from her own flask into her mouth, then closed her bottle. "If we make it to the top, maybe we can melt some snow."

"Hey! Look up here!" Yara called from a ledge a little way above them. "I've found something."

Tom clipped his flask back on

to his belt and followed Elenna towards Yara and Queen Aroha. They were staring into a dark, narrow tunnel that led into the rockface.

"If we go this way, we can cut off a chunk of the climb," Yara said.

Elenna frowned. "How can you possibly know where the passage leads, if no one's been here in five hundred years?" she asked. "We're just as likely to get lost inside the mountains and die."

"If it means rescuing Rotu sooner, surely it's worth taking the chance," Yara said. "And we won't get lost if we remember our turnings. Or is fierce little Elenna afraid of the dark?"

Elenna turned to Yara, her eyes flashing with fury. "I am not— "

Queen Aroha cut her off. "If it might be a quicker route, I think we should take it," she said. "We have already angered Zargon by not leaving the jewels. I can't bear to think how he might be punishing Rotu for that."

Remembering the cruelty in the wizard's gaze, Tom had to agree with the queen. "I can use my yellow jewel to help me memorise the route we take," he told Elenna, tapping the belt of magic gems around his waist. "And the entrance looks far too small for a Beast to enter." Tom pushed his sweaty hair back from his face, suddenly longing for a bit of cool shade. "If nothing else, it'll get us out of the sun!"

"Fine," Elenna said. She picked up what looked like a length of weathered animal bone from the mountainside, then tore a strip of cloth from her pack. "But let's at least take a light with us."

After lighting her makeshift torch with her flint, Elenna dipped her head, and stepped inside the tunnel. Yara and Aroha quickly followed. As Tom ducked into the darkness behind them, he found the narrow tunnel mouth opened out into a good-sized passage. The air was cool, but instead of relief, Tom only felt a creeping dread. The dank staleness reminded him of a dungeon. *Or a crypt.*

The bobbing flame of Elenna's torch cast flickering shadows across the tunnel walls as she walked with long strides, head held high – clearly trying to show Yara that she wasn't afraid.

But Tom was growing steadily more and more uneasy as the light from the tunnel mouth faded. The skin on the back of his neck tingled. He turned again and again, straining his eyes to see in the gloom, listening hard, half-expecting to hear footsteps that weren't their own.

Suddenly, he did hear something – a soft sigh, almost like a breath. The chill air stirred, making the flame of Elenna's torch dance. They all stopped dead, listening.

Yara looked around, wide-eyed.

"What was tha—"

A deep booming rumble echoed up from beneath their feet, drowning her words. Another breeze swirled around them, cold and dank. Elenna's torch flickered and went out. In the sudden darkness, Tom heard a clattering, rattling sound… tiny pebbles skittering down the tunnel walls. His chest tightened.

"What's going on?" Yara asked fearfully.

The floor trembled. Tom staggered as another rumble filled the tunnel.

"Earthquake!" Tom cried, lifting his shield to protect his head from falling rocks. "We have to go back!" But as he turned, a tremendous crash

greeted him, along with a whoosh of air. A torrent of stones pummelled his body, almost forcing him to his knees as choking dust filled his lungs. Someone let out a yelp of pain. "The ceiling's collapsed behind us!" Tom told the others, just as the tunnel floor bucked, and more chips of rock rained down on his shield. "Run!" he cried.

They all tore away through the blackness, stones pattering down all around them. Tom kept his shield raised, blindly following the tunnel. From behind, he could hear more crashes and booms; and from ahead, the sound of huge rocks slamming to the tunnel floor. *We're going to be crushed!* Tom plunged on through the darkness, expecting at any moment that the ceiling would fall.

"This way!" Elenna cried from a short distance ahead. "I see a light down this shaft!" Tom could just make out her shape in a faint glow of daylight, and those of Yara and Aroha behind her. They threw themselves into the side tunnel. As Tom raced after them, the mountain gave a tremendous shudder, sending another torrent of rocks tumbling. Beyond the running forms of Elenna, Yara and the queen, the crack of light ahead grew steadily smaller as rubble blocked the entrance. Tom's heart clenched.

We're going to be buried alive!

THE PEAKS OF DESPAIR

Tom's breath burned in his chest with the effort of running. Grit filled his mouth and nose, and the sound of falling rock echoed around him as he raced towards the exit. Relief coursed through his veins as he saw first Yara, then Elenna duck through the narrow gap and out into daylight. Suddenly the tunnel gave a mighty judder. *CRASH!* Huge chunks of rubble smashed to the ground around Aroha. The queen stumbled sideways with a yelp, then staggered back to her feet.

Tom could see that their exit would be blocked any moment. Calling on the magical speed of his golden leg armour, he surged forwards, barrelling into the queen and sending her flying out into daylight. Tom leapt through the opening after her, and turned just in time to see the whole cave ceiling fall with a thunderous crash, spewing out clouds of dirt and chips of stone.

For a long moment, everyone stood

gasping for breath, their faces grey with stone dust. A purple bruise already bloomed on Aroha's cheek, and they all had bleeding scratches, but no one seemed badly injured.

Elenna rounded on Yara, speaking through clenched teeth.

"So much for your shortcut," she said. "We almost died!"

Yara shrugged. "But we didn't. And look..." She pointed to the towering peak now behind them. "We've avoided all that climbing."

Yara was right. But, looking up at the snow-capped summits, far above with many sharp crests in between, Tom knew they still had a long, hard climb ahead.

After they'd all taken sips from their water bottles, Aroha and Yara took the lead, with Elenna next, and Tom behind. They made slow but steady progress, wedging their fingers and toes into tiny crevices in the rock and pulling themselves upwards. Tom kept himself a little way behind the others so he would have time to react if anyone lost their grip. The rays of the sun hammering down on his head and shoulders began to feel like physical blows as he climbed. Looking up, Tom couldn't help envying Elenna. Lighter and more agile, she moved as gracefully as a wildcat. She turned her head and gazed back at him, waiting for him to catch up.

"You know, I'm really starting to have doubts about Yara," Elenna whispered, once Tom was level with her.

"How so?" Tom managed to ask

between panting breaths.

“Well, she’s supposed to be a bodyguard, but she didn’t wait to help her queen when the ceiling collapsed in that tunnel. And remember how she tried to take charge of the jewels? It just all seems a bit odd."

"Well, she certainly seems to have a knack for almost getting herself killed, and us along with her," Tom said, wiping the sweat from his brow on his sleeve. "But that's just bad luck. And it was dark in the tunnel. I don't think she could have done much to help Aroha. The queen really trusts her."

"I still think it—" A scream cut Elenna off, and Tom looked up to see Yara hanging by one hand beside Aroha, her other hand and her feet scrabbling to find a hold on the sheer rockface. Before Tom could reach for the shield on his back,

Aroha shot out a hand and caught hold of Yara's cloak. Yara quickly found a foothold and started to climb once more.

"Maybe she's just clumsy?" Tom said. "After all, I can't believe she did that on purpose. It would be too risky."

"Either way," Elenna hissed, "she's a disaster waiting to happen, or a traitor. Whichever it is, she doesn't belong on this Quest!"

They climbed onwards into the afternoon, scrambling over sharp crests of rock only to find still higher peaks ahead. Eventually, they reached a plateau, wider than any they had passed so far. Aroha shrugged off her pack and sat down beside it.

"We'll take a short rest here," she said, pushing her sweaty hair back from her face. Elenna and Yara sank to the ground. Tom did the same, grateful for the chance to recover. Every muscle in his body ached, and his arms felt like lead weights. But before he could unclip his water bottle, a shiver ran through the rock beneath him. The skin on his scalp tightened as the familiar patter of falling stones reached his ears.

CRACK!

Tom leapt to his feet, staring in horror as a slender fissure opened in the ground nearby. "Watch out!"

he shouted. Elenna and Aroha leapt aside as the widening crevasse zigzagged towards them.

"My bag!" Aroha cried, as the ground lurched once more. Her pack, which had been resting right on the lip of the opening, toppled over the edge. Halfway to her feet, Yara made a grab for it but missed, overbalancing to teeter on the edge of the crevasse. Tom lunged and grabbed her cloak, yanking her backwards.

They huddled together, their backs pressed against the shuddering rock that edged the plateau as the ground continued to tremble. At last, the vibrations eased to a stop.

"That was close!" Tom said. But Aroha shook her head, her eyes wide with horror.

"You don't understand..." she said. "The jewels were in my bag!"

They all stepped to the edge of the narrow crevasse and looked down. The walls were craggy and uneven, with jagged overhangs and sharp points of stone jutting from the rock. Tom spotted Aroha's backpack lying on a narrow shelf way below them.

"Elenna, give me the rope," Aroha said. "Lower me down." Tom was about to offer instead, when Elenna piped up.

"I'll fetch them," she said. "I'm the lightest, so you'll be able to lower me down most easily."

Tom nodded. "You're right," he said. "But we'll take it slow."

After Elenna had tied the rope around her waist, Yara, Aroha and Tom each took hold of it, Yara in front and Tom at the back. As Elenna eased herself into the narrow opening and disappeared over the lip, Tom gradually let the rope run through his hands, bracing himself against her weight. Aroha and Yara each took up the slack in turn, slowly lowering Elenna until their rope was almost paid out.

"I've got the bag," Elenna called. "You can pull me up!"

"Right," Tom told Aroha and Yara,

“when I say ‘pull,’ we all tug together.” They both nodded. “Pull!” Tom said. All three of them heaved on the rope, passing a section through their hands. Tom’s hands soon felt raw from the heat of it. Each time he gave the

word, they hauled Elenna higher. Working together, they made quick progress, and soon, judging by the coil of rope behind him, Tom knew Elenna had to be close to the top.

"Wait!" she called, and Tom froze

at the sharpness of her tone. "The rope keeps catching on the rock. It's fraying. You'll have to take it really— "

Yara tugged sharply on the rope, then stumbled backwards into Aroha, the cord suddenly, horribly slack. Aroha fell against Tom, and he braced his feet to steady her, at the same time as he heard Elenna let out a piercing scream which tore at his heart.

1

A DANGEROUS RESCUE

"Elenna!" Tom cried, a cold horror crashing over him. He rushed to the edge of the chasm and looked down, expecting the worst – Elenna's broken body far below. He let out a sigh of relief when he spotted his friend crouching against the rockface on the narrow shelf where the jewels had

landed, the frayed rope dangling from her waist.

"I'm all right!" Elenna called up, unbending slowly and brushing grit from her hands.

"Can you climb out?" Queen Aroha

called down from Tom's side.

Elenna ran her eyes over the wall of rock, and gripped hold of a ridge above her head; but when she started to pull herself up, her hands slipped. She tried once more, grunting with effort, but again fell back.

"The rock's too smooth down here," she called.

Tom glanced at the pile of rope they still had left and gritted his teeth in frustration. *It's too short!* He racked his brains, trying to think of another way to reach Elenna. A hideous groan interrupted his thoughts as the rock beneath him shunted forward. Tom staggered back to catch his balance, but the ground lurched again – and then again. Bracing himself against the juddering movement, he looked towards the chasm, and gasped.

It's beginning to close!

Shuffling to the edge, Tom peered down to see Elenna staring up at him, her pale face and wide eyes shining in the gloom.

"Help!" she cried as, with another grating rumble, the rockfaces jolted closer together.

"Elenna!" Yara called, crawling on her hands and knees to the lip of the chasm. "Throw me the jewels before it's too late!"

Tom could hardly believe what he was hearing. "No!" he shouted, his voice hoarse. He scanned the moving rockfaces, looking for any way to help his friend… He spotted a narrow split in the far wall, a few arm-spans down. *That might just work!* Snatching up the remains of the rope, Tom drew his sword, and in one swift, desperate motion, he leapt down into the chasm, ramming his blade point-first into the gash. A shock jolted up his arm, wrenching his muscles as his sword took his weight…and held!

Dangling from his sword, his body shaking with the motion of the rock, Tom let the rope unfurl. *Please let it reach!* The crevasse walls ground closer together, casting Elenna's face into deeper shadow as the end of the rope fell towards her. It stopped short.

"Jump!" Tom told her. Elenna glanced up, her brows knitted together. Tom felt a stab of worry – *It's too high!* But then Elenna gritted her teeth, bent her knees and leapt.

Tom felt the wrenching tug of his friend's weight on his arms as she caught the rope firmly and held tight, then began to climb. His chest and arms screamed with a pain as if he was being torn in half, but he kept a tight grip on his sword and on the rope as Elenna drew closer. Finally, she reached him. Tom clamped his teeth together as his friend climbed over him and then onwards, up the trembling rockface.

"Catch hold of my hands!" Aroha called. Tom glanced up to see the queen and Yara now on his side of the closing chasm. The queen lay on her stomach reaching down for Elenna while Yara clung to her waist, steadying her. Elenna grabbed hold of Aroha's outstretched arms. Aroha and Yara pulled. With only a slender crack remaining, Elenna scrambled free. She turned at once, reaching her own arms down towards Tom.

"Hurry!" Elenna screamed, her face etched with horror. Tom's arms burned and he could hardly catch his breath, but with one last burst of effort, he wrenched his sword from the rock, and forced himself to climb. His strength was almost spent, but somehow he grabbed Elenna's hand. Aroha gripped his wrist too. Together they pulled. Tom pushed with his legs and tumbled free of the groaning earth, out into the daylight just as the crack in the ground slammed shut behind him with an echoing *BOOM!*

Tom lay still, gasping for breath. Then he pushed himself up to sitting. He could hardly tell where the fissure in the mountain had been. His gut clenched with a wave of sickness as he thought of what would have happened to Elenna or him if…

He shook his head. *It won't help the Quest to think like that.*

Elenna was already on her feet. She rounded on Yara, her face white with fury and her hands balled into fists. "That is the last straw!" Elenna growled. "I told you to go slow with the rope. You almost got me killed – again! And you were just going to leave me in there to be crushed as long as you had the jewels..."

"How dare you?" Yara spat. "You risked Rotu's life, as well as the safety of Tangala, by keeping the jewels. You only care about your own pathetic hide. You have cast doubt on my honour one too many times now, and I will not stand for it any

longer..." Yara drew her sword and fell into a fighting stance, glaring at Elenna. "I challenge you to a duel!"

"Oh, so you *do* have a sword?" Elenna said, her eyes wide and mocking. "I was beginning to think that scabbard was just decoration. After all, you didn't use it against Akorta, did you? No wonder Rotu got kidnapped. With a bodyguard like you, who needs enemies?"

Yara let out a screech of rage and lunged, with deadly intent – but Aroha stepped between the feuding pair.

"Stop!" she said. "I order both of you to— "

ROOAAAAR!

The whole mountain shook with a violence that snatched the breath from Tom's lungs. He flattened himself to the ground, dust and debris filling his vision. He threw his arms over his head, scree raining down, pummelling his body as the bruising, bone-jolting tremors went on and on.

We're going to be smashed to pieces...

Then, all at once, the earth fell still. Silence rang in Tom's ears. He slowly lifted his head, wincing at the pain in his arms, his back, even his legs, and shuffled up to sitting. Through a haze of rock dust, he saw Elenna staggering to her feet nearby. Then he spotted Queen Aroha on her knees, staring into a new chasm right before her, her face as white as parchment.

"Yara..." the queen said weakly,

pointing into the crack. Tom's mouth dropped open as the terrible truth dawned on him. He pushed himself to his feet, crossed to the chasm, and

looked down. Straight, smooth sides dropped away below him, plunging downwards into darkness. There was no sign of Yara at all. He turned to Aroha, seeing his own horror echoed on her face.

"She's gone," Aroha said.

THE QUEST CONTINUES

"No! She can't be!" Elenna cried. "We have to help her! Give me the rope."

Tom shook his head, trying to ignore the sickly feeling in his chest. "There's no bottom that I can see," he told Elenna. "No one could survive a drop like that."

Elenna looked stricken. "I didn't… I didn't mean…" Her voice shook, and tears spilled down her cheeks.

"It's not your fault," Tom told her. "It was just a terrible accident. And Yara knew the risk she was taking in coming here. She died a warrior's death."

Queen Aroha still sat by the crevasse, frozen with sorrow.

Tom went to her side and put a hand on her shoulder. "It's not safe to stay here," he said. "Yara wouldn't want us to give up hope. She would have wanted us to save Rotu. The best way to honour the memory of a warrior is to finish what they have started." A sudden memory of his father, also lost to a Quest, sent a piercing pain through Tom's heart. "We need to rescue your nephew and make sure Zargon never gets his hands on those jewels," he managed to say.

Aroha turned to him, her face as still and blank as a mask. "Maybe Yara was right about the jewels," she said, her voice small and distant. "Maybe we should just leave them here, and go back to Avantia. Yara's dead…Elenna almost perished. How many more lives need to be lost over an ancient kingdom no one has even set foot in for five hundred years?"

"This isn't about Vakunda, or even Rotu any more," Tom said, firmly. "This is about the safety of the whole of Tangala, and Avantia too. If we leave the jewels for Zargon, we will be giving an enemy the power he needs to defeat us. We must go on. And I'm sure Yara would have said the same…”

The queen looked up at him, and her eyes seemed to focus.

“You are right, Tom,” she said. She clenched her jaw, her expression hardening. “I am queen of Tangala and Avantia. The Quest must go on. But I won’t forget Yara’s sacrifice. Zargon will pay.”

Tom took the lead as they all climbed onwards in silence, weary with grief. High, jagged outcrops of rock crowded close together in every direction, interspersed with treacherous, unstable slopes. The terrain became snowy as Tom picked his way upwards, trying to find a route through. But time and again, paths that had looked clear turned out to be blocked with rubble, forcing them to turn back, only to find a deep gully where Tom felt certain there had been firm rock only a short while before.

Clambering up a steep incline sandwiched between two sharper peaks, Tom found yet another jutting wall of icy stone blocking their way. With a growl of frustration, he turned. Then he gasped at the sight of a sharp ravine cut across the base of the rocky slope they had climbed just moments ago. "We never crossed that ravine," he murmured. "It's like these mountains are alive! How can we find a way over them when everything keeps changing?"

Stones clattered to the ground somewhere below them. "Who's there?" Tom cried. But in response, he heard only the mocking echo of his own voice. Everything was still and silent. A graveyard of cold, dead stone and ice.

Elenna drew her bow from her back and aimed an arrow down the slope. "Something's up here," she said. "I can feel it too."

A breathy, rumbling growl, almost too low to hear, echoed around them. His pulse quickening, Tom brandished his weapon as Aroha drew her own blade. The three of them scanned the rocky terrain.

Tom flinched when something gooey and wet hit the back of his neck. A stench like rotting flesh filled his nostrils. He looked up, straight into the huge eyes of a colossal dog, crouching ready to leap down from the rocky ledge. Vast muscles bulged beneath the creature's snow-white pelt, and saliva dripped from gleaming fangs, each as long as a dagger – and easily as sharp.

Tom swallowed, his mouth suddenly dry.

Lycaxa!

6

LYCAXA

"Look out!" Tom called to Elenna and Aroha, throwing himself out of the Beast's path as Lycaxa leapt, his huge paws swiping through the air. He caught a glimpse of Aroha's wide, panicked eyes before both she and Elenna dived away from the Beast's slashing claws.

Tom landed awkwardly, feeling

the rock shift beneath him, and started to roll faster and faster down the steep slope. Sharp stones jabbed into his sides, and the sky and ground spun in his vision. He threw out his legs and arms, trying to slow his fall, and finally came to a stop right at the edge of the gully. He shook his head to clear the dizziness and leapt up to see the Beast crouched over the prone body of Aroha. The queen's eyes were closed, and her leg stuck out at a sickening angle.

Tom measured the distance he'd need to cover to reach her. *Lycaxa will snatch Aroha up in his jaws before I can get there!*

Beyond the Beast, he spotted Elenna peering from behind a pillar of rock, a bloody gash on her forehead, and her eyes fixed on the Beast's massive, muscled form. The huge dog-Beast loomed over the queen, his vast head sweeping from side to side, his nostrils flared – trying to catch a scent.

Why doesn't he attack? Tom wondered. Then, as he caught sight of the Beast's pale eyes, cloudy and clotted like cooked egg white, he realised something. *Lycaxa's blind!*

Tom lifted a hand, waving to get Elenna's attention. As she glanced towards him, he pointed at the Beast then put his hand over his eyes, miming blindness. Elenna's own eyes widened in understanding, and she nodded. Tom put a finger to his lips, and she nodded again; then she slowly, silently fitted an arrow to her bow. But as she took aim, her foot shifted, nudging a rock. With a throaty growl, the Beast twisted to face her, ears swivelling and nostrils flaring. Then he started to prowl slowly forwards, ears pricked. Elenna smiled, and drew back her bowstring, aiming straight for the monster's broad chest.

Then Aroha stirred, hissing with pain.

No, no, no…

Tom winced as Lycaxa swung away from Elenna and leapt towards the queen. Elenna loosed her arrow. *Thwack!* It struck the rippling muscle of the Beast's flank, lodging there. Lycaxa stumbled and let out a howl. Twisting his body, the Beast snatched at the arrow with his teeth, growling as he tore it from his flesh. Tom took the chance to slip past on tiptoe, his heart in his mouth, barely daring to breathe. He sank down beside the queen, putting a finger to his lips.

Her face grey with pain, Aroha pointed to her leg. *Broken*, she mouthed. Tom glanced towards the Beast. Lycaxa was standing alert once more, his head turning slowly, drool dripping from his jaws as he cast around for the scent of his prey. Tom silently slipped the green jewel from his belt and handed it to the queen.

Clenching her teeth against the pain, Aroha touched the gem to her injured leg. Beyond the Beast, Elenna had already readied another arrow. Tom caught her eye, then mimed shooting away from the Beast, up the slope. Elenna nodded, and Tom raised his hand, palm forward, signalling for her to wait. He slipped off his boots, slowly unbent and crept towards Lycaxa.

As he drew close, he made out the taut lines of every bulging muscle beneath Lycaxa's pelt. The vast dog-Beast was taller than any carthorse, and even broader across his barrel

chest. His powerful jaws and dagger teeth looked strong enough to bite through rock, and each giant paw was tipped with curved grey claws, as sharp as scythes.

Lycaxa turned, his ears tilting

forwards. Tom froze, his heart hammering, but the dog-Beast's sightless stare moved on, scanning the rocky slope. *He doesn't know I'm here!* But still his body thrummed with tension, ready to run. Turning to Elenna, Tom nodded once. She aimed her arrow up the slope, in the opposite direction, and let it fly.

The arrow clattered off a rock. Lycaxa sprang, leaping high and landing on the rock with a growl of rage. The Beast snarled and snapped, raking at the stone with his claws, crunching up chunks of stone, then spitting them out until only a pile of rubble remained. Then Lycaxa stood panting, his ears pricked once more and his snout twitching as he hunted his victims' scent.

Creeping up behind the massive hound on the balls of his feet, Tom drew back his sword to strike. But at the faint whistle of the blade cutting

air, Lycaxa snarled and kicked out with his powerful hind legs. Pain exploded in Tom's chest as the mighty blow landed, catapulting him into the air…

THE CANYON OF DEATH

Tom landed hard on his back, his head smashing against the rocky ground. He gasped and retched, curling into a ball as his bruised lungs struggled to draw air. Through the mist of his pain, he saw the Beast prowling towards him, flanks heaving with angry breaths, and his blind eyes narrowed with hate. Despite his bulk, the massive hound's slow movements were eerily silent.

Clutching his aching ribs, Tom gulped down the pain and nausea rising inside him. He knew that to groan, or even to breathe, would mean death at the jaws of Lycaxa...

Maybe I can reason with him.

He edged his hand slowly towards the red jewel in his belt. As soon as his fingers touched the familiar stone, he sensed the Beast's rage and hunger, as well as something else... Arrogance. Cruelty. The clammy revulsion Tom felt reminded him at once of Zargon, and his hope dwindled. *But I still have to try.*

Lycaxa, he called to the Beast with his mind. *We are not your enemy. We mean you no harm. All we want is safe passage across the mountains. We will leave you in peace if you just let us pass.*

A harsh angry bark of laughter answered him. *Foolish human boy*, the Beast sneered. *Nothing crosses my mountains. Not ever!*

Tom clenched his teeth. Calling on the strength of heart from his golden chainmail, he forced his aching body to uncoil. Slowly, silently, he rose into a crouch, his sword lifted before him. *Very well*, Tom told the Beast. *In that case, you will perish!*

Glancing around, Tom quickly spotted Aroha, sitting, but still looking woozy. Near to the queen, Elenna had an arrow trained on Lycaxa's bulky frame, but Tom caught her eye and shook his head to signal to her: *Arrows will only enrage him further… I have to finish this. Now.*

With a nod, Elenna relaxed her bow.

Drawing on the speed from his golden leg armour, Tom broke into a run, dashing past the Beast and up the craggy slope, away from his friends. Sensing Tom's presence, Lycaxa snarled. Tom glanced back to see the dog-Beast leap into a run, barrelling after him up the slope. Lycaxa let out a sharp, angry bark, and the ground right before Tom dropped away, splitting open into a deep chasm. Tom gathered himself and leapt, flying over the crevasse

and landing in a run on the other side. Another furious bark echoed from behind him. Ahead, with a crashing roar, a pillar of rock shot upwards from the slope, blocking Tom's path. Going too fast to stop, Tom threw himself sideways, his mind reeling with shock. *The Beast is doing this! He's been playing with us all along*, Tom realised. He dodged past the jutting stone, then gulped when he saw more pushing upwards from the slope ahead of him – huge, towering formations, thrusting skywards.

Slaloming right and left through the thicket of stones, Tom glanced back to see the dog-Beast close behind him, bounding effortlessly over the shaking ground. Fear clutched Tom's heart. *Even with the magic of my leg armour, Lycaxa is faster…* He raced on, leaping another widening split in the ground, then gasped, his stomach suddenly left behind as the rock beneath him surged upwards, carrying him aloft. He dug his heels into the rock, windmilling his arms, somehow managing to stop himself plunging to his death, and looked down. Far below, Lycaxa paced between the jutting stones, muzzle to the ground and ears twitching in the sudden quiet. *He's lost my scent!* thought Tom.

Come out and fight, puny human! Lycaxa growled in Tom's mind.

Tom touched the red jewel in his belt. *I have no quarrel with you*, he answered. *I ask you again: let us pass and we will leave you in peace. You have my word...*

Never! Lycaxa roared.

Then I have no choice but to end this now, Tom told the Beast. He nudged a small stone with his foot, pushing it off the pillar. It tumbled down, hitting the ground with a *clink*.

ROAR! Lycaxa pounced on the tiny rock, snapping his massive teeth and slashing his claws at the ground.

Tom lifted his sword and leapt. *Now you're finished!* He landed on Lycaxa's broad back and brought

his blade down point-first between the Beast's muscled shoulders, gasping at the shock of the impact – it was like trying to stab granite. His sword bit through Lycaxa's thick hide but lodged shallowly in the Beast's flesh. With a howl of fury, Lycaxa bucked, tearing Tom's grip from his sword and throwing him into the air.

Tom landed on his side and skidded over the rocky ground, coming to a stop only a hand's breadth from one of the Beast's crevasses. Glancing over the edge, Tom shuddered. The bottom of the fissure was studded with deadly-looking spears of rock. *That was far too close*, he thought, as he felt the hope draining from him.

But when he saw Lycaxa scenting the air, his vast head raised, Tom began to get a new idea...

HANGING ON

Wincing with pain, Tom got to his feet. "I'm over here, dog breath!" he shouted.

Lycaxa snarled with a fury that sent saliva flying from his jaws. Tom held his ground, his gut clenched in terror as the vast muscled dog-Beast hurtled towards him, vicious teeth bared. At the last possible moment,

Tom leapt aside. Lycaxa sped past him, letting out a strangled yelp as he fell. Tom turned to see a point of rock drive straight through the creature's heaving flank, impaling him. Lycaxa howled in agony, his massive paws

scrabbling at the air as his body convulsed.

It worked! Tom stared, unable to look away from the horrible sight of the Beast's frantic movements slowing down, his breath coming in

ragged huffs, as bloody foam flecked his muzzle. A wave of pity crashed over Tom. *What a terrible way to die*. But then he heard Lycaxa's voice in his mind – a venomous growl, filled with hate.

If I must die, then so will you! The Beast let out a hideous high-pitched whine. With a sound like ice cracking, Tom felt the lip of the chasm give way beneath his feet. His stomach flipped. He twisted as he fell, reaching desperately for the chasm wall, the rock skinning his palms. He managed to grip a narrow ledge with one hand, and then the other, his fingertips just hooking over the tiny ridge. He closed his eyes, willing himself not to fall, his fingers already slick with sweat and screaming with pain.

I can't hold on! I'm going to die!

"Help!" he cried, hoarsely, terrified that even the effort of shouting might cause him to fall. He heard the clatter of footsteps and felt hope flare in his chest.

"Hey!" A voice called from above him. Tom opened his eyes and looked up, expecting to see Elenna or Aroha – but it was Yara's face that greeted him.

"You're...alive!" Tom gasped.

Yara nodded, a strange, hungry light in her eyes. "Do you have the jewels?" she asked. "Throw them up

here! We can't risk losing them!"

Tom gaped up at her, hardly able to find words. "No, I don't have the jewels," he managed at last. "I'm clinging on for my life! Do you think you could give me a hand?" A flicker of irritation crossed Yara's face, and terror knifed through Tom's chest at the thought she might just leave him there.

"Tom!" Elenna cried, her face appearing over the lip of stone above, along with Aroha's. Moments later, their strong arms were reaching down for him, tugging at his wrists, pulling him to safety.

Tom caught his breath, then got to his feet. He turned to gaze down at the Beast along with the others. Lycaxa lay still now, his paws reaching out stiffly, and his blind eyes closed.

"He's defeated," Aroha said. She put a hand to the bag on her back.

"The jewels!" she said. "I can feel them vibrating." As Aroha drew the pouch of gems from her bag, Tom saw a warm yellow glow through the material. The queen took out an amber-coloured stone, pulsing with light. She held the jewel up, and with a gentle sigh like a summer breeze, Lycaxa's bulky form dissolved into a saffron-coloured mist that streamed into the yellow jewel, leaving Tom's sword lying among the rocks. The gem glowed brightly once more, like a tiny sun, then went dark.

"I guess the Beast is at peace now," Tom said.

"We did it!" the queen said,

beaming. "And Yara's back!" Aroha threw an arm around her countrywoman. "I thought you were dead. How did you survive?"

Yara shrugged. "I was knocked out when I fell. I came to in a cave and followed a tunnel until, eventually, I found my way out... I've been looking for you – and when I heard all the noise, I came to help. Looks like I got here just in time!"

Just in time to miss the whole battle! Tom thought. He saw Elenna frowning as she watched Aroha hug Yara. *She could have saved me... But all she wanted was the jewels. Elenna's right...*

Before Tom could voice his

concerns, the ground began to tremble again, and his stomach churned with dread. *Not another earthquake*... But the trembling felt different this time, more like a gentle hum. Tom's vision blurred – or the landscape did. He blinked to see points of pale green grass sprouting from rich earth, and the sharp peaks of the mountain range softening into rolling hills. His sword now lay on a small hummock by his foot, tiny blue and white flowers peeking from the grass all around it. Rushes grew along the edge of a glittering stream nearby. Tom picked up his weapon, and looked at his friends to see them all

gazing about in wonder.

"A hare!" Elenna said, pointing. Sure enough, Tom spotted the little brown creature nibbling at the grass near a tree covered in blossom.

Aroha drew in a deep breath of fresh air and smiled broadly.

"We're winning!" she said. "We're getting closer to Zargon, and we've defeated two of his Beasts – which means there are only two more to go. Once we've defeated them, we will reach Zargon's prison, and rescue Rotu!"

"We're sure to succeed!" Yara said. "And now that we have a chance to rest, and to replenish our stores, we will be stronger than ever for the next stage of our Quest."

But as Yara and Aroha set off towards the stream, side by side, Tom and Elenna exchanged a troubled look. *We still need to get past two more of Zargon's Beasts*, Tom thought, *as well as the wizard himself. We're lucky to be alive as it is.* He let out a deep sigh. *And I can't help thinking that, with Yara on the Quest beside us, we might have more to reckon with than just Evil Wizards and Beasts…*

He hoped he was wrong.

THE END

CONGRATULATIONS, YOU HAVE COMPLETED THIS QUEST!

At the end of each chapter you were awarded a special gold coin. The QUEST in this book was worth an amazing 8 coins.

Look at the Beast Quest totem picture opposite to see how far you've come in your journey to become

MASTER OF THE BEASTS.

The more books you read, the more coins you will collect!

Do you want your own Beast Quest Totem?

1. Cut out and collect the coin below
2. Go to the Beast Quest website
3. Download and print out your totem
4. Add your coin to the totem

www.beastquest.co.uk

READ THE BOOKS, COLLECT THE COINS!

EARN COINS FOR EVERY CHAPTER YOU READ!

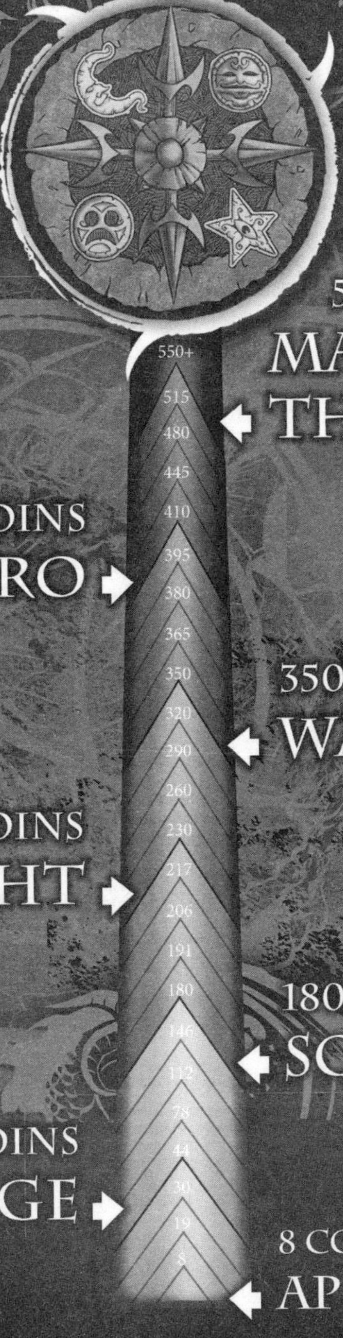

550+ COINS
MASTER OF THE BEASTS

410 COINS
HERO

350 COINS
WARRIOR

230 COINS
KNIGHT

180 COINS
SQUIRE

44 COINS
PAGE

8 COINS
APPRENTICE

550+
515
480
445
410
395
380
365
350
320
290
260
230
217
206
191
180
146
112
78
44
30
19
8

READ ALL THE BOOKS IN SERIES 25:

THE PRISON KINGDOM!

Don't miss the next exciting Beast Quest book: GLAKI, SPEAR OF THE DEPTHS!

Read on for a sneak peek...

THE LEGEND OF THE JEWELS

Tom and Elenna sat opposite Queen Aroha and Yara in the warm halo of light created by their campfire. The hills behind them echoed with the last calls of birds settling to roost, and the evening sky was a deep blue scattered with stars. The queen held the four Jewels of Tangala in one hand. She tilted them towards the flames so that rich flashes of colour shot through the polished gems. Yara, bodyguard to the queen's kidnapped nephew Prince Rotu, gazed intently at the jewels. They all waited for Aroha to begin her tale.

Tom eased himself down to rest his elbow on his pack. After a good supper of dried meat he felt almost refreshed from their earlier battle against Lycaxa. The fearsome hound was the second Beast they had defeated on their Quest to rescue Rotu from Zargon. The Evil Wizard had demanded the jewels in exchange for the prince, so Tom was eager to find out more about the magical gemstones.

Aroha's face was half hidden in flickering shadow, but her eyes shone as she met each of their gazes in turn before beginning her story.

"Once, many centuries ago, a Tangalan queen called Nala held a tournament to find herself a husband and consort, as was the custom in those days. It was a grand occasion, with much merrymaking, but not everyone was happy." The fire popped loudly. Aroha paused as a branch settled lower in the flames, then she went on.

"Unbeknownst to the queen,

the Royal Goldsmith, Davron, had fallen in love with her. Driven mad by jealousy, he created a crown for the new husband inlaid with jewels that he had enchanted with a curse. Though the consort had been a good and honest man, the jewels made him hunger for power, twisting his mind until he wanted the kingdom for himself."

At Aroha's side, Yara nodded vigorously. "He even tried to murder the queen," she said, "but Nala's maid stopped him. She was named the queen's official bodyguard, as a reward for her loyalty and bravery."

Aroha dipped her head. "That's right," she said. "On his arrest, the disgraced consort's crown was removed, and the curse was lifted from him. Horrified by what he had done, the poor man begged his queen for forgiveness. Nala began to suspect the jewels and confirmed her suspicions by trying on the crown herself. Having great wisdom and strength of character, the queen was able to resist the jewels' power, but she felt their pull enough to realise where the evil lay. She locked the jewels away, vowing that they would never see daylight again."

"It's a shame they didn't stay hidden," Tom said. "How did Zargon get his hands on them?"

Aroha frowned down at the

gleaming stones in her palm and let out a sigh. "Unfortunately, the jewels are so powerful that even under lock and key, they still call to those with evil in their hearts. Zargon was pulled to the magical gemstones. He stole them, and, as you know, created the Kingdom of Vakunda with its four Realms: jungle, mountains, river and palace – each with a Beast to protect them."

Tom gazed at the gemstones. Though the flames of their campfire had burned down to a smouldering glow, the jewels still pulsed with a light from within. "It's amazing to think that four small gems could create a whole kingdom!" he said.

“And then cause the very same kingdom to transform into a treacherous wasteland,” Elenna added, pulling her cloak tighter about her. “It looks like they have the power to create and to destroy.”

Aroha nodded. “When the four Jewels of Tangala were taken back from Zargon five hundred years ago, they sucked all the goodness out of Vakunda. This turned them into the perilous landscapes we have been crossing. Somehow, by vanquishing Zargon’s Beasts, we are reversing that process.”

Tom thought of how the treacherous jungle and the Peaks of Despair had changed after they had defeated the Beasts that guarded them. The jungle had become lush and beautiful, and the jagged mountain range had transformed into the gently rolling Hills of Plenty – but not before almost claiming their lives. The glowing embers of the fire spat out a shower of sparks, the flames now almost gone. Tom glanced about at the darkness pressing in on them and felt suddenly cold.

"We should get some rest," he said. "Tomorrow will be a long day."

Tom stretched himself out beside Elenna, using his pack as a pillow. Aroha and Yara did the same, wrapping themselves in their travelling cloaks to keep out the chill of the night. But, as Tom tried to settle, a nagging unease kept prodding him awake. He couldn't help thinking of the strange, almost hungry light in Yara's eyes as she had watched the jewels in Aroha's hand. He turned to see Elenna still awake and alert too.

"Do you think we should keep a watch?" Elenna whispered. "I have a horrible feeling Yara's up to something."

Tom nodded. "I know what you mean. The way she keeps disappearing when we need her most, and trying to get her hands on the jewels… I'll take first watch," he said, though his eyes felt gritty with exhaustion. He glanced across at Yara, already snoring softly, then folded his arms on his chest.

Whatever you're up to, we'll get to the bottom of it.

Yara slept soundly through Tom's shift, and he swapped with Elenna halfway through the night. The next morning, he woke to a shadowy landscape wreathed in silver-grey mist, and Elenna's hand on his shoulder. "Did anything happen?" he asked her, pushing himself up to sitting.

Elenna grinned. "Apart from you

snoring like a hog?" she said. Beyond the ashes of their fire, Yara shifted in her sleep, and Elenna's smile vanished. She shook her head. "She didn't stir. But I still think we should be wary."

Read

GLAKI, SPEAR OF THE DEPTHS

to find out what happens next!

Meet three new heroes with the power to tame the Beasts!

MEET TEAM HERO

FROM ADAM BLADE

TEA... UK

DARE TO BE DIFFERENT